MOON TROUBLE

by M. C. Helldorfer

illustrated by Jonathan Hunt

Bradbury Press • New York

Maxwell Macmillan Canada   Toronto
Maxwell Macmillan International
New York   Oxford   Singapore   Sydney

Bradbury Press
Macmillan Publishing Company
866 Third Avenue
New York, NY 10022

Maxwell Macmillan Canada, Inc.
1200 Eglinton Avenue East
Suite 200
Don Mills, Ontario M3C 3N1

Macmillan Publishing Company is part of the Maxwell Communication
Group of Companies.

First edition
Printed in the United States of America on recycled paper
10 9 8 7 6 5 4 3 2 1

The text of this book is set in Galliard.
Typography by Julie Y. Quan

LIBRARY OF CONGRESS CATALOGING-IN-PUBLICATION DATA
Helldorfer, Mary-Claire, date.
Moon trouble / by M. C. Helldorfer ; illustrated by Jonathan Hunt.
—1st ed.
p.   cm.
Summary: When the moon falls into Farmer Klank's river, every
attempt to get it back into place fails, until Paul Bunyan is
called.
ISBN 0-02-743517-2
1. Bunyan, Paul (Legendary character)—Juvenile fiction.
[1. Bunyan, Paul (Legendary character)—Fiction. 2. Moon—Fiction.
3. Tall tales.] I. Hunt, Jonathan, ill. II. Title.
PZ7.H37418Mo   1994
[Fic]—dc20   92-22233

For Isabel Walcott Ladd,
with thanks for all your encouragement
—M. C. H.

To Dennis and Karen Hunt, who have helped
in more ways than they know to keep the "moon shining."
—J. H.

Now, this happened in the East, where they have low, grassy hills with brick cities planted in between, where few folks have ever seen cloud-poking pine trees, much less the giant logger Paul Bunyan. Most thought Paul was just a good story.

Until that evening the moon splashed down in the river.

The ducks got excited. Farmer Klank's son heard them and came running from the house, his mother and sister right behind.

"Look here," said Boy Klank. "Duck's laid an egg big as a pony. I'm going to ride this hatchling right out to sea."

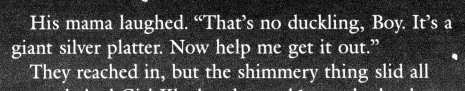

His mama laughed. "That's no duckling, Boy. It's a giant silver platter. Now help me get it out."

They reached in, but the shimmery thing slid all around. And Girl Klank, who took more baths than a fish, said, "Mama, I believe it's a lovely cake of soap!"

HILDEGARDE II

About then Farmer Klank came puffing in from green-bean field, his old neighbor Turpentine beside him. Klank leaned over the riverbank. He glimpsed a face. His own got pale as a ghost. "Anybody we know die?"

"Not a soul," Turpentine replied. Then he squinted up at the sky. It was cluttered with stars, nothing but stars. "Looks to me, folks, like you got yourself a moon."

Well, Klank rang the big bell, and neighbors came from all around. When they fished out the glisteny thing, sure enough, it was the moon.

They tried maybe a hundred different ways to get the moon back in the sky. Some folks tied it to kites. But it was so heavy, nobody could run fast enough to set it sailing.

The children strung together five balloons. But there was none of that special gas around to send the moon laughing upward.

So they rolled it on some blankets. Everybody picked
up an edge and made like a trampoline. *Heave!*
The moon soared and spun.

Then, look out! *Moon tumbling down.*

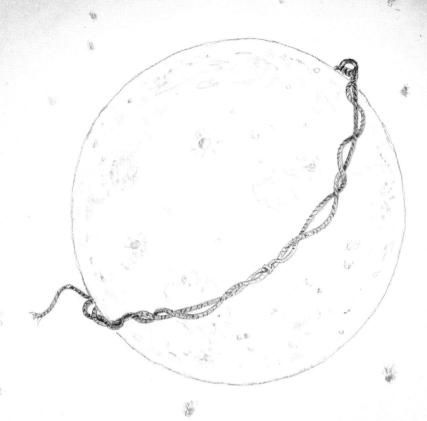

The children caught it in their blankets and threw it back up again. Up, down. Up, down. Along the coast tides rose and fell with the moon, leaving fish in people's window boxes.

Try as they might, the neighbors couldn't get the moon high enough to stick. Old Turpentine said, "Best we call Paul Bunyan."

Now, some scoffed, for, like I said before, Easterners haven't seen many wonders. Few believed Turpentine's stories about his days in Paul's logging camp.

But night was growing awfully dark. So they sent out a pigeon, and before you could say *moon trouble*, Paul came with Babe, his big blue ox.

He said some how-dos, then tossed the moon to
Babe. Babe caught it with a hoof and kicked it to the
sky. What a pretty arc it rode, shining yellow, then
white, climbing on up the darkness.
Then, look out! *Moon dropping!*

From upriver came a splash that sent showers to the coast. Paul waded in and plucked out the moon. "Who here's got a slingshot?" he asked.

Nobody had one big enough for him, so they set about making it. Turpentine, who was feeling younger than a hundred and six that day, shinnied up a tree and cut off all but its two big limbs.

Paul tied some snakes together.

Twang, those vipers sang when Paul let go and
the moon shot up. It scattered stars left and right,
knocking a few sparklers to earth.

Everyone cheered. They all thought the moon had
stuck. But, look out! *Moon rolling down.*

And Paul said, "I guess there's no way but one. Now, when I call 'Hold on,' you all gotta hold on." Then he and Babe headed north.

All the sudden the ground started moving, rolling left, rolling right. Paul was up the North Pole, hanging on to the earth's axis like a sailboat mast, swinging it left, swinging it right.

"Hold on!" he hollered.

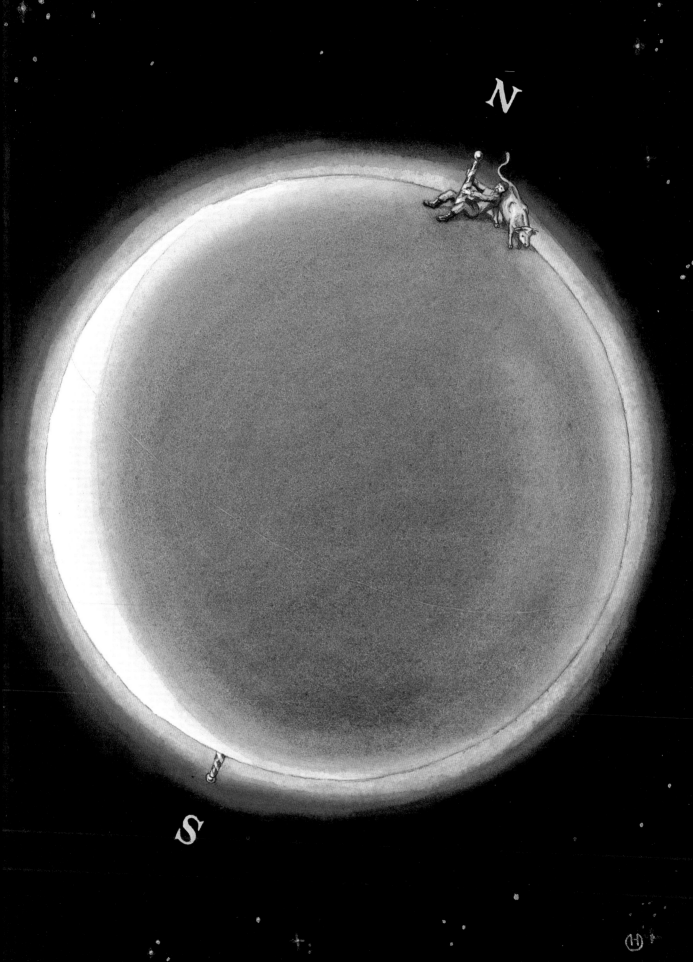

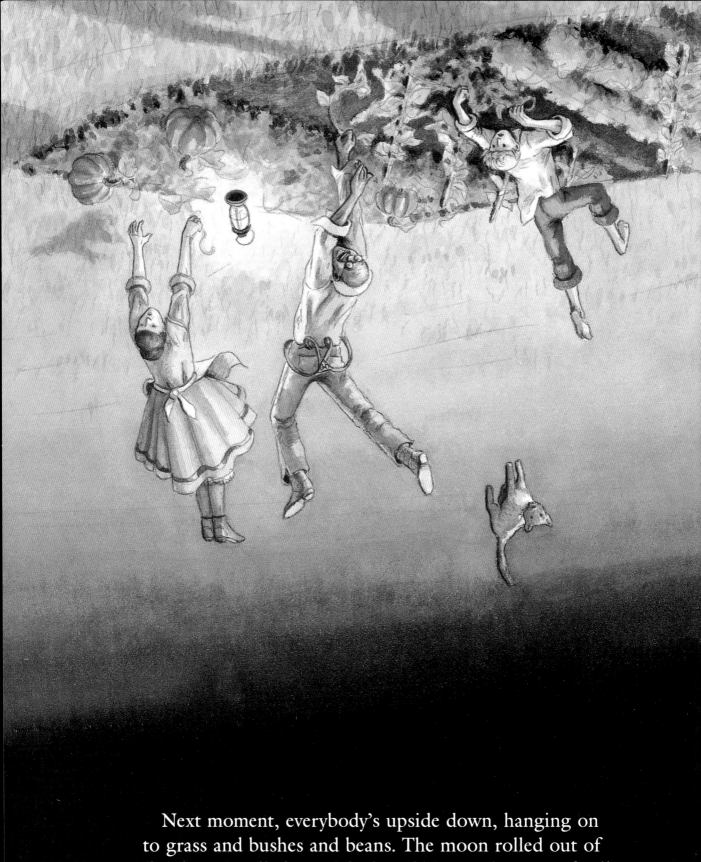

Next moment, everybody's upside down, hanging on
to grass and bushes and beans. The moon rolled out of
the river. It rolled past Klank and Turpentine, past family
and friends, all hanging like balls on a Christmas tree.
Suddenly, the world swung right side up again.

The moon slid down in the West. The sun pushed up in the East.

Then it was day, of course, but nobody felt much like working. So everybody went swimming and waited to see if the moon would rise again.

It did, with a little fish tagging behind.